IS THE DEVIL A GENTLEMAN?

BY

SEABURY QUINN

British Library Cataloguing-in-Publication Data
A catalogue record for this book is available from the
British Library

CONTENTS

SEABURY QUINN

Seabury Grandin Quinn was born in Washington D.C. in 1889. In 1910, he graduated from law school, and was admitted to the District of Columbia Bar. He served in World War I, and after his Army service became editor of a group of trade papers in New York. His first published work was 'The Law of the Movies' (1917), in *The Motion Picture Magazine*, and his first published fictional story was 'Demons of the Night' (1918), in *Detective Story Magazine*. He introduced the occult detective Jules de Grandin as a character in 1925, and continued writing tales about him until 1951. Quinn's stories were incredibly popular, and between the twenties and fifties he appeared in *Weird Tales* magazine more times than both Robert E. Howard and H. P. Lovecraft. His novel *Roads* was also widely read. Quinn died in old age on Christmas Eve.

IS THE DEVIL A GENTLEMAN?

It had been a day of strange weather, a day the calendar declared to be late April and the thermometer proclaimed to be March or November. From dawn till early dark the rain had spattered down, chill, persistent, deceptive, making it feel many degrees colder than it really was, but just at sunset it had cleared and a sort of angry yellow half-light had spilled from a sky of streaky black against a bank of blood-red clouds. Now, while the dying wind was groping with chill-stiffened fingers at the window-casings, a fire blazed on the study hearth, its comforting rose glow a gleaming island in the gathering shadows, its reflection daubing ever-changing pattern on the walls and tightly-drawn curtains.

'On such a night,' the Bishop quoted inexactly as he helped himself to brandy, 'mine enemy's dog, though he had bit me, I would not turn away from my door.'

Dr. Bentley, rector of St. Chrysostom's, dropped a second

lump of sugar in his coffee and said nothing. He knew the Bishop, and had known him since their student days. When he quoted Shakespeare he was really searching through the lumber rooms of memory for a story, and there were few who had a better store of anecdotes than the Right Reverend Richard Chauncey, missionary, soldier, preacher and ecclesiastical executive, worldly man of God and godly man of the world. He'd looked forward to Dick's coming down for confirmation, and had made a point of asking Kitteringson in to dinner. Kitteringson was all right, of course; good, earnest worker, a good preacher and a good churchman, but a trifle too—how should he put it?—too dogmatic. If you couldn't find it in the writings of the Fathers of the Church or the Thirty-nine Articles he was against a proposition, whatever it might be. A session with the Bishop would be good for him.

'Good stuff in the lad,' thought Dr. Bentley as he studied his junior covetly. A rather strong, intelligent face he had, but marked by asceticism, the face of one who might be either an unyielding martyr or a merciless inquisitor. Now he was leaning forward almost eagerly, and the firelight did things to his earnest face—made it look like one of those old medieval monks in the old masters' paintings.

'I've been wondering all day, sir,' he told Bishop Chauncey, 'what you meant when you told the confirmation class they should use common sense about religious prejudices. Surely, there may be no compromise with evil—'

'I shouldn't care to lay that down as a precept,' the Bishop answered with a low chuckle. 'We're told the Devil can quote Scripture for his purposes; why shouldn't Christians make use of the powers of darkness in a proper case?'

Young Dr. Kitteringson was aghast. 'Make use of Satan?' he faltered. 'Have dealings with the arch-fiend—'

'Precisely, son. Shakespeare might have been more truthful than poetical when he declared the Prince of Darkness is a gentleman.'

'I can't conceive of such a thing!' the younger man retorted. 'All our experiences tell us—'

'All?' cut in Bishop Chauncey softly, and the young rector fell hesitant before the level irony of his gaze. 'How old are you, son?'

'Thirty-two, sir, but I've read the writings of the Fathers of the Early Church, and one and all they tell us that to compromise with evil is a sin against—' He stopped, a little abashed at the look of tolerant amusement on his senior's face, then: 'Can you name even one case when compromise with evil didn't end disastrously for all concerned, sir?' he challenged.

'Yes, I think I can,' the Bishop passed the brandy sniffer back and forth beneath his nostrils, inhaled the bouquet of the old cognac appreciatively, then took a delicate, approving sip. 'I think I can, son. Like you, I have to call upon my reading to sustain me, but unlike you I can't claim ecclesiastical authority for my writers. One of them, indeed, was an ancestor of mine, a great-grandfather several times removed.'

The gloom that waited just beyond the moving edge of firelight seemed flowing forward, like a slowly rising, stagnant tide, and a blazing ember falling to the layer of sand beneath the burning logs sent a sudden shaft of light across the intervening shade, casting a quick shadow of the Bishop on the farther wall. An odd shadow it was, not like the rubicund, grey-haired churchman, but queerly elongated and distorted, so that it appeared to be the shade of a lean man with gaunt and predatory features, muffled in a cloak and leaning forward at the shoulders, like one intent—almost in the act of pouncing.

Kundre Maltby (said the Bishop, drawing thoughtfully at his cigar so its recurrent glow etched his face in alternate red highlight and black shadow) was a confessed witch, and witches, as you know, are those who have made solemn compact with the Evil One.

She was a Swedish girl—at least she claimed that she was Swedish—whom Captain Pelatiah Maltby had found somewhere in his travels, married, and brought back to

Danby by Salem. Who she really was nobody knew.

Captain Maltby's ship, the *Bountiful Adventure*, came on her Easter Monday morning, clinging to a hatch-grating some twenty miles or so off the Madeira coast. He'd cleared from Funchal the night before, swearing that he'd never make the port again, for the Portuguese had celebrated Easter with an *auto da fé* at which a hundred condemned witches had been burned, and the sight of the poor wretches' sufferings sickened him. When he asked the castaway her name she told him it was Kundre, and said her ship had been the *Blenkinge* of Stockholm, wrecked three days before.

Maltby marvelled at this information, for he had been in the Madeiras for a whole week, and there had been no storm, not even a light squall. But there the girl was, lashed to the floating hatch-top, virtually nude and all but dead with thirst and starvation. Moreover, she had very winning ways and more than a fair share of beauty, so Captain Maltby asked no further questions, but put in at New York and married her before he brought the *Bountiful Adventure* up the coast to Danby.

Their life together seems to have been ideal, possibly idyllic. He was a raw-boned, tough-thewed son of New England, hard as flint outside and practical as the multiplication tables within. But it was from such ancestry that Whittier and Holmes and Bryant and Longfellow sprang, and probably beneath his workaday exterior Pelatiah Maltby had a poet's soul. They had twin children, a boy and a girl. At Pelatiah s insistence the girl was named for her mother, but Kundre chose the name of Micah for the boy, for in the whole Scripture she liked best that Prophet's question, 'What doth the Lord require of thee, but to do justly, and to love mercy, and to walk humbly with thy God?'

She took to transplantation like a hardy flower, and grew and flourished on New England soil. From all accounts she must have been a beauty in a heavy Nordic way, a true woman of the sea. Full six feet tall she was, and strong as any man, yet with all the gracious curves of womanhood. Her hair, they say, was golden. Not merely yellow, but that metallic shade of gold which, catching glints of outside light, seems to hold a light of its own. And her skin was white as sea-foam, and her eyes the bright blue-green of the ice of the fjords, and her lips were red as sunset on the ocean when a storm has blown itself away.

Prosperity came with her, too. The winds were always favourable to Captain Maltby's ship. He made the longest voyages in the shortest time. When other ships were set upon by tempests and battered till they were mere hulks he came safely through the raving storms or missed them altogether, and his enterprises always prospered. Foreign traders sold him goods at laughably low prices, or bought the cargoes that he brought at prices that astonished him.

He brought back treasures from the far corners of the earth, silks from Cathay and Nippon, carved coral from the South Sea Isles, pearls from Java, diamonds from Africa, a comb of solid beaten gold from India—and the golden comb seemed pallid when she drew it through the golden spate of her loosed golden hair.

The neighbours were first amazed, then wondering, finally suspicious. Experience had taught them Providence dealt even-handedly with men and balanced its smiles with its frowns. Yet Pelatiah Maltby always won. He never had to drain a cup of vinegar to compensate him for the many heady cups of the wine of success he quaffed.

It was Captain Joel Newton who brought matters to a head. He and Captain Maltby had been rivals many years. His pew was just across the aisle from Maltby's in the meeting house, his wife sat where she could not help but see the worldly gewgaws Maltby lavished on Kundre, and Abigail Newton's tongue had an edge like that of a new-filed adze, and her jealousy the bitter bite of acid. Joel Newton heard himself compared to Pelatiah Maltby, with small advantage, every Lord's Day after service, and, driven by the lash of a shrew's tongue, he determined to find the key to Maltby's constant success, and set himself deliberately to trail the *Bountiful Adventure* from one port to another.

Not that it helped him. The *Bountiful Adventure* outsailed him every trip, and when he came into a foreign berth he found that Maltby had been there before him, secured what trade there was, and sailed away.

They came face to face at last at Tamatave in Madagascar. Maltby had traded rum and salted fish and tobacco for a holdful of rich native silver, and the local traders had no thought of laying in new stocks for months. Newton's ship was loaded to capacity with just the wares that Maltby had disposed of so profitably, there was no market for his cargo, his food was running low, and ruin stared him in the face.

Both had taken more of the French wines the inn purveyed than was their custom. Maltby was flushed with success, Newton bitter with the mordancy of disappointment. 'Had I a witch-woman for wife I'd always fare well, too,' he told his rival.

'How quotha?' Maltby asked. 'What meanest, knave? My Kundre is the fairest, sweetest bloom—'

'As ever sank its taproots deep in hell,' his rival finished for him, 'Oh, don't 'ee think to fool us, Neighbour Maltby! We know what 'tis that always sends the fair winds at thy tail when others lie becalmed. We know what 'tis that makes the heathen take thy wares at such great prices, and pay thee ten times what thou'd hoped to get. Aye, and we know whence comes thy witch-mate, too—how the Papishers had burned a drove of warlocks in the Madeiras the day before ye found her floating in the ocean. She said her vessel had been wrecked three days before, but had there been a storm? Thou knowest well there had not. Did'st offer her free passage back to the island, and did she take thy offer kindly?'

Now this was a poser, for Pelatiah had offered to set Kundre on shore at Funchal when he rescued her, and she had refused tearfully, and begged him to hold to his course.

'And why?' asked Captain Newton as he warmed to his task of denunciation. 'I'll tell 'ee why, my fine bucko—because she was a cursed witch who'd slipped between the Papists' fingers and made use of thee to ferry her to safety. Thinkest thou she loves thee? Faugh! While thou'rt away she wantons it with every man 'twixt Danby and old Salem Town——'

'Thou liar!' The scandalous words were like to have been Joel's last, for Pelatiah drew his hanger and made for him with intent to stab the slander down his throat with cold steel, but Joel was just a thought too quick.

Before his rival reached him he jerked a pistol from his waistband and let fly, striking Captain Maltby fairly in the chest. Afterwards he boasted that it was a silver bullet he had used, since, as everybody knew, witches, warlocks and were-beasts were impervious to lead, but vulnerable to silver missiles.

However that might be Captain Maltby halted in midstride, and his hanger fell with a clatter from his unnerved hand. He hiccoughed once and tried to draw a breath that stopped before he had it in, sagged at the knees, fell on his side and died. But with that last unfinished breath they say he whispered, 'Kundre dearest, they have done for me and will for thee if so be that they can. God have thee in His keeping—'

Maltby, of course, was a Protestant, and the only Christian cemetery in the town was Catholic. It was not possible a heretic should lie in consecrated ground, but the missionary priest took counsel with the rabbi of the little Jewish congregation and arranged to buy a grave-site in the Hebrew burying ground.

There was no ordained minister of his faith to do the final service for Maltby, so the priest and rabbi stood beside his grave, and one said Christian prayers in Latin, and the other Jewish prayers in Hebrew, while the grim-faced sailors from New England stood by and marvelled at this show of charity in those they had been taught to hate, and responded with tear-choked 'A-mens' when prayers were done and time had come to heap the earth upon the body sewn in sailcloth in lieu of a coffin.

It was a Wednesday in mid-April when the killing took place, and Kundre, so the story goes, was sitting beside the brooklet that ran through her back-lot. The weather was unseasonably warm, and her children waded in the stream and searched for buds of ground-rose while she sunned and bleached the hair that was her greatest pride—or vanity, according to the neighbours' wives. Suddenly she raised her head like one who listens to a hail from far away, shook back her clouding hair and cupped one hand to her ear to sit there statue-still for a long moment. Then, with a cry that seemed to be the echo of her riven heart-strings' breaking, she called out, 'Pelatiah! Oh beloved!' and fell forward on her face beside the brooklet, lying with her arms outstretched before her like a diver's when he strikes the water, while her great, heroically-formed body twitched and jerked, and little, dreadful moans came bubbling from her lips, like blood that wells and bubbles from a mortal wound.

Presently she rose and dried her eyes and went into the house where she laid away her gown of crisp blue linen and put on widow's weeds before she sought Ezekiel Martin the stone-mason and ordered him to cut and set a gravestone in the village churchyard. You could see that tombstone now if you should go to Danby burying ground. It reads:

Sacred to the memory of
PELATIAH MALTBY
Chriſtian man & feacaptain
Moſt foully done to death by jealouſie
at Tamatave in Madagaſcie

Now, you'll allow it would be cause for comment, even in these days when extrasensory perceptions are taken as more or less established facts, for a woman to become aware of her husband's death half-way round the world from her at the very moment of its happening. The circumstances caused comment in mid-seventeenth century New England, too, but not at all of the same kind. Everybody dreaded sorcery and witchcraft then, and in every unexplained occurrence men saw Satan's ungloved hand. So when Kundre went forth in her mourning clothes, sorrowing dry-eyed at the empty grave where she had placed the tombstone, neighbours looked at her from beneath lowered lids, and when she went to divine service at the meeting house the tithing man went past her hurriedly, and hardly paused to hold the alms basin before her, though he knew it would be heavier by a gold piece minted with the symbol of King Charles' majesty when he withdrew it.

In August came the *Bountiful Adventure* with her ensign flying at half-mast, and Captain Maltby's death was confirmed by the sorrowing seamen.

But what became of Captain Joel Newton and his ship the *Crystal Wave* nobody ever knew. He had set sail from Tamatava the same day he shot Maltby, for everyone agreed he had provoked the quarrel, and the commandant of the garrison threatened his arrest unless he drew his anchor from the harbour-mud at once. The rest was silence. Neither stick nor spar nor broken bit of wreckage ever washed ashore to show the *Crystal Wave's* fate, or that of Captain Joel Newton and the twenty seamen of his crew.

Voyages of a year or even two years were the rule those days, and it was not until King Charles had been beheaded and the Lord Protector proclaimed that Abigail Newton descended from the 'widow's watch' that topped her square-roofed house beside the harbour and changed her home-spun gown of blue for one of black linsey woolsey, then sent for Zeke Martin the mason to cut and set a stone in Danby churchyard.

The twenty widows of the *Crystal Wave's* crew also went in mourning, and bewailed their joint and several losses piteously. When they passed Kundre in the street they looked away, but when she'd gotten safely past they spit upon the ground and muttered 'witch!' and 'Devil's-hag!'

Kundre was a Swedish woman, and though the good folk of Danby had small use for King James's politics and even less for his religion, they were with him to a man in his views on witchcraft. Moreover, they recalled how Scandinavian witches had raised storms and tempests to prevent the Princess Anne from reaching Scotland where her marriage to King James was to be solemnized, and some of the more learned in the village knew the legends of *Sangreal* and remembered that the temptress who all but kept the Holy Grail from Parsifal was named Kundry. There seemed little difference between her name and Kundre's. Kundry of the legend was a witch damned past redemption, might not Kundre—the strange outland woman who knew of her husband's death four months before the news came home—also be a potent witch?

It seemed entirely possible and even probable, and when the widowed Abigail met widowed Kundre in the village street and taxed her with destroying both the *Crystal Wave's* master and crew by witchcraft, something happened to confirm the worst suspicions.

'Thou art a wicked, Devil-vowed and wanton witch!' said Abigail in hearing of at least three neighbour women. 'By thy vile arts thou raised a monstrous storm and sank the *Crystal Wave* and all her people in the ocean.'

Kundre looked at her, and in her ice-blue eyes there seemed to kindle a slow light like that which the aurora borealis makes on winter nights. 'Thy tongue is dipped in venom like a serpent's, Goody Newton,' she replied in the deep voice which was her Nordic heritage. 'It never wags except to hurt thy neighbours, so 'twere best thou never used it hereafter.'

Whether from the look in Kundre's eyes, or from astonishment that anyone should dare to tell her to keep still we do not know, but it was amply attested that Abigail for once had no reply to make, and we find in the old town records of Danby that on the evening after this encounter she lost her power of speech completely. More, she lost the use of her tongue, for it swelled and swelled until she could not keep it in her mouth, and she could take no nourishment but liquids, and those with greatest difficulty.

In the light of present-day medical knowledge it would not be too difficult to attribute her misfortune to that rare condition known as macroglossia or hypertrophy of the tongue, which doctors tell us is due to engorgement and dilation of the lymph channels. Most of us who have served in hospitals have seen such cases, where the swollen tongue hangs from the mouth and gives the patient a peculiarly idiotic look. But medicine was far from an exact science those days, and besides there was the testimony of the women who had seen the curse of silence laid on Abigail. Three hours after sunset Kundre was 'spoken against' as a witch and duly lodged in Danby jail.

By the common law of England torture was forbidden to force a prisoner to accuse himself, but by the witchcraft statutes of King James certain "tests" which differed from torture neither in degree nor kind were permitted. One of these was known as "swimming," for it was believed a witch's body was so buoyed up with evil that it could not sink in water.

Accordingly, upon the second day of her confinement Kundre was brought out to be "swum." Stripped to her shift they led her from the jail to the horse-pond which served the village as reservoir and ornamental lake at once, forced her to sit cross-legged on the ground and tied her right thumb to her left great toe, her right great toe to her left thumb with heavy linen thread which had been waxed for greater strength, and to make it cut more deeply in the tender flesh. Then over her they dropped a linen bed-sheet, tumbled her all helpless as she was upon her side and tied the sheet's loose ends together, exactly as a modern housewife makes a laundry bundle ready. A rope was fastened to the knotted sheet and willing hands laid hold on it and dragged it out into the water.

Now here we have a choice between the natural and the supernatural. We have all seen the properties of wet cloth to retain the air and resist water. The device known as water wings with which so many children learn to swim is simply a cloth bladder wet before inflation, and as long as outside pressure is evenly applied it will support surprisingly large weights in calm water.

Perhaps it was as natural a phenomenon as this that kept the accused woman afloat on the calm surface of the village horse-pond. Perhaps, again, it was something more sinister. At any rate, the sheeted bundle bobbed and floated on the quiet surface of the pool as easily as if it had been filled with cork, and a great shout went up from the spectators 'She swims! She swims; it is the judgement of just Heaven; she is a proven witch!'

Her trial lasted a full day, and people came from miles about to hear the evidence poured on her. Ezekiel Martin the stonemason told how she came to him and ordered him to cut the tombstone for a man whose limbs were scarcely stiff in death, though none could know that he had died until his ship came a full four months later.

There was no dearth of testimony concerning the fine winds and weather that had been her husband's portion since he married her, or concerning the storms that had plagued his rivals.

Abigail Newton stood up in court that all might see her swollen tongue, and though she could not speak, she went through an elaborate dumb-show of the way the curse had been laid on her. Less reticent, Flee-from-the-Wrath-to-Come Epsworth, Rebecca Norris and Susan Clayton told under oath how they had seen and heard Kundre strike Abigail with speechlessness.

A tithe of such evidence would have been enough to hang her, and the jury took but fifteen minutes to deliberate upon their verdict, which, of course, was guilty.

Asked what she had to say in her defence before the court

pronounced sentence, she made a seemly curtsey to the judge and answered without hesitation ' 'Tis true I am a witch as ye have charged me. Long years agone my sire and dam made compact with the Prince of Evil and bound me by their covenant, but never have I used my power to hurt a living creature, brute or human. That I should wish my man to prosper was but natural. Thus far I used my power over wind and tides, but no farther. Whether Heaven punished Goodman Newton for the foul murder that he did on my poor man I cannot say. I know naught of the matter, nor did I lift a finger to bring Heaven's retribution on him. "Vengeance is mine, I will repay," saith the Lord.

'As for the swollen tongue of von shrew, belike it is the malice of her black and jealous heart that bloats it. As to that I cannot answer; but hark ye, neighbours, if I had the power to release her I'd not use it. The town is better for her silence, as I wis ye all agree.'

With that she made another curtsey to the judge and stood there silent, waiting sentence: 'Since, therefore, Goodwife Kundre Maltby hath by her own confession admitted she was justly tried and convicted, so let her on account of her bond with the Devil and on account of the witchcraft she hath practised, be hanged by the neck until she be dead.'

The usual formula in hanging cases was for the court to add, 'and may God have mercy on thy soul,' but such a sentiment seemed obviously out of place here, and the judge forbore to express it.

They carried out the sentence next day, and a mighty crowd was gathered for the spectacle. The members of the trained band were much put to it to control the rabble when the hangman drove his cart beneath the gallows tree and made the hemp fast to her neck.

She wore her widow's weeds to execution, and round her neck was clasped a slender chain of some base metal with a flat pendant like a coin hung from it. It was the only ornament she'd had when Pelatiah found her floating on the grating, and she had laid it by when they were married. Now, through a whim, perhaps, she chose to wear it at her death.

They'd let her children visit her in jail the night before, and she had sent the girl back for the bauble. 'Look well on it, my sweet,' she told the child when it was clasped about her neck. 'The time may come when thou'lt have need of it, and if it comes thou shalt not cry for it in vain.'

As the hangman bound her elbows to her sides before he slipped the noose beneath her chin she begged him, 'Leave the worthless chain in place when thy grim task is done, good Peter Grimes. In my left shoe thou'lt find a golden sovereign hidden to repay thee for thy work. Take it and welcome, but if thou take'st the chain and pendant from me—a witch's curse shall be on thee.'

Peter Grimes was a poor man, and the clothes a felon stood in when he died were part of his perquisites, but he had no stomach for a witch's curse, so when he found the gold piece in her shoe as she had promised he took it and was well pleased to leave the worthless chain in place.

She did not die easily, from all accounts. Her splendid body was too powerful, the tide of life ran too strong in her, so she dangled, quivering and writhing in the air a full five minutes. Then Peter Grimes, perhaps in charity, perhaps because he wished to have the business over with and go home to his breakfast, seized her by the legs and dragged until the double burden of his weight and hers proved too much for her spinal column, and with a snapping like the cracking of a fire-dried stick her neck broke and her struggles ended.

They raised the stone that she had set above her husband's empty grave, scooped out a shallow opening beneath it and dropped her in, coffinless and without proper graveclothes. So, as the neighbours sagely said, she had outreached herself and ordered her own tombstone when by her wicked wizardry she had the tidings of her man's death at the instant it occurred.

And here again we're forced to make a choice between the natural and the supernatural. That Kundre should have confessed she was guilty was not particularly important.

We know that under heavy mental stress people will accuse themselves of almost any crime. There's hardly a sensational murder case in which the police don't have to deal with numerous entirely innocent self-accusers. That part of it is understandable.

What is more difficult to explain is that at the very moment Peter Grimes broke Kundre's neck the swelling in Abigail Newton's tongue began to subside, and by noon she had entirely regained the power of speech. Indeed, she regained it so fully that within six months she was twice sentenced to the ducking-stool for public scoldings, and finally was forced to stand before the meeting house on the Sabbath with a muzzle on her face and a paper reading 'Common Scold' hung by a string around her neck.

Not the least mystifying thing about the mystery of Kundre Maltby was the way her fortune disappeared. That she and Pelatiah had been rich was common knowledge, but when the assessors went to her house to take her property in custody they could find nothing of substantial value. Not a single gold or silver coin, nor yet a bit of jewellery could they turn up, though they searched the place from cellar to ridgepole and even knocked down several walls in quest of concealed hiding places. So, balked in the attempt to work a forfeiture of her fortune, they sold the house and land at public vendue, put the proceeds in the town treasury and farmed the children out to be taught useful trades.

Micah was apprenticed at the rope-walk owned by Goodman Richard Belkton, Kundre took her place among the sewing maids of Goodwife Deborah Stiles, and except when they were in school or went, well chaperoned, to divine service at the meeting house, they never saw each other.

Their lot was not a happy one. We all know the sadistic cruelty of the young. The lad who goes to a new school today has a hard time until he's proved himself to be the equal of the class bully, or till the novelty of hazing him wears off. But Kundre and her brother had to face the taunts and insults of their classmates endlessly. No one wished to sit with them or share a hornbook with them. If, maddened by the spiteful things said of his mother, Micah fought his tormentor and came off winner, his victory was vociferously attributed to witchcraft. If he lost the fight the victor called on all to witness how Heaven had helped the right in overcoming evil.

Both were apt pupils, but their readiness in reading, ciphering and writing caused no commendation from the schoolma'am. She too believed their aptitude infernally inspired and made no secret of it. So successful recitations were rewarded by an acid reference to their mother's compact with the Evil One. Failure brought a caning.

In all the dreary monotone of life the one highlight for

Kundre was Hosea Newton. It may seem strange that the son of her mother's fiercest persecutor should prove her only friend, but it was no stranger than the contrast between Hosea and his mother. Where she was angular and acid and sharp-tongued he was inclined to plumpness, slow of speech and even-tempered. When all the little girls drew their skirts back from Kundre as from diabolic pollution, he chose a seat beside her on the form, and shared his primer with her and, to the scandal of the class, often gave her tidbits from the ample luncheon which his mother packed for him each morning. When Charity Wilkins accused Kundre of stealing a new thimble from her he found the missing bauble concealed in Charity's pocket and pulled her hair until she admitted her fault. Charity's big brother Benjamin took up the lists for his sister, whereupon Hosea entered combat with enthusiasm and left Benjamin with a bloody nose and greatly chastened tongue.

But this little interlude of friendship had disastrous results. Goodwife Wilkins went to Abigail, who, horrified that her son had espoused the witch-child's cause, took him forthwith to Reverend Silas Middleton, who quoted Scriptual texts to him—'Evil communications corrupt good manners'—exhorted him, prayed over him and finally caned him soundly.

After that Hosea had to content himself with smiling

at Kundre over his primer. All speech between them was forbidden, and though the Reverend Middleton's precepts had made but small impression on Hosea, he had a vivid memory of the thrashing that accompanied them.

The quiet of the lazy years flowed over Danby like a placid river. In the harbour the tall ships shook out their wings and sped to the far corners of the earth and presently came back again with holds filled with strange merchandise. Or perhaps they did not come back, and the women put on mourning clothes and there were new stones in the churchyard, with empty graves beneath them. King Philip's War was fought and won and the settlers needed to fear Indian raids no longer. But in the main life just went on and on. Its groove was deepened, but the course and pattern never changed.

Hosea Newton went away to Harvard College where he was to be trained for the ministry, Micah worked at the rope-walk, harbouring black resentment in his heart, but not daring to give tongue to it; Kundre toiled in Goody Stiles's workroom from sunrise to sunset. She proved a clever needle-woman and her work was eagerly bought up, but had no credit for it. Goodwife Stiles displayed the dresses proudly, and accepted compliments with modest grace, but she never told whose agile fingers fashioned them. In this she showed sound business sense, for many of her customers would have hesitated to wear garments made by a witch-child. And then—

One evening in late summer Kundre lay in Goodman Stiles's oat field. She had worked all day, her eyes and muscles ached, and she was so tired that she could have cried with it, but now she had a little respite. The earth felt warm and comforting to her cramped muscles, she seemed to draw vitality from it while a little breeze played through the bearded grain, making it rustle softly, like a bride's dress.

A bride's dress! Kundre thought. Other maids went to the meeting house or stood up in their own homes in stiff, rustling taffety while the parson joined them to the men of their choice. Was she forever doomed to tread the earth in loneliness, to find no lover, no friend, even, in the whole world? It seemed a hard fate for a maid as well-favoured as she.

Kundre knew that she had beauty. Unlike her mother, she was little; little and slender with grey eyes and a soft-lipped, rather sad smile. Her hair, despite the severe braids in which she wore it, was positively thrilling in its beauty. Paler than her mother's, it had the sweet amber-gold of melted honey in dark lights and the vivid sheen of burnished silver when the sunshine fell on it. There was a sort of aristocratic fragility hinted at by her arched, slender neck and delicately-cut profile, her hands were so slight that she wore child's mittens in cold weather, and the cast-off shoon of neighbours' half-grown daughters were too large for her, even when she wore the thickest woollen stockings.

But now she had kicked off the rough brogans and stripped the heavy cotton stockings off and drew her naked, gleaming feet up under her as she half sat, half lay upon the warm and friendly earth. She rested her elbow upon a bent knee, outlining her chin with her fingers as she looked toward the blue, distant hills. How would it seem, she wondered, to have someone look at her in friendship, speak a kindly word to her, perhaps—her pulses quickened at the daring thought—tell her she was beautiful?

A footstep sounded at the margin of the field and she crouched like a little partridge when it hears the hunter coming. If she were very still, perhaps whoever came would pass her by unseeing. She had no wish to be seen. Since early childhood she had never known a friendly look or word, except—

The footsteps came still nearer, swishing through the nodding grain, and now she heard a man's voice humming softly:

Wish and fulfilment can severed be ne'er,
Nor the thing prayed for come short of the prayer—

'I crave thy pardon, mistress!' Unaware of Kundre crouching in her covet he had almost trodden on her. A flush suffused his face as he stepped backward hurriedly and almost lost his balance in the process.

'I had no business trespassing on Neighbour Stiles's land—why, Kundre, lass, is't truly thou? How lovely thou art grown!' he broke off in surprised delight and to her utter blank amazement, dropped down to the ground beside her. 'It must be full three years since I have seen thee,' he added.

Kundre looked at him in wonder. At first it had been but a man she saw, and men, almost as much as women, were her natural enemies, for she had led an odd and hunted life, and like an animal knew the world of men and women only through the blows it dealt her. But as she looked into the smiling friendly face she felt the blood flow into her cheeks and bring sudden warmth to her brow, for it was Hosea Newton sitting by her in the oat field, Hosea Newton's voice, all rich with friendly laughter, asked how she did, and—her heart beat so that she could hardly breathe—Hosea Newton has just said that she was lovely.

The years had been kind to him. Strongly made, wide-shouldered, he was still not burly, only big; and his face was undeniably handsome. He had a short upper lip and a square jaw with a dimple in it, blue eyes set wide apart beneath dark, curving brows, and lightly curling dark hair that fitted his well-formed head like a cap.

'Art glad to see me?' he asked frankly, and Kundre sat in thoughtful silence for a while before she answered softly:

'I am not sure, Hosea. In all the world thou art the only person who has spoken kindly to me since my mother— died—but once, I recollect, thou suffered for thy kindness to me. Now—'

'Now,' he mimicked laughing, 'I'll dare the parson or the elders to admonish me. I am my own man, Kundre, and think what thoughts I choose, say what I will and go with whom I please. Aye,' he added as she answered nothing. 'I've thought a deal about things, Kundre, and what I think might not make pleasant hearing for the parson and the elders, or my mother, either. I've seen the Quakers whipped and hanged and branded for their faith's sake, seen helpless, innocent old women go tottering to the gallows tree for witchcraft that they never worked, and could not work, and seen the men who call themselves God's ministers work lustily in Satan's vineyard.'

'Thou thinkest, then—' she asked him with a quaver in her voice—'it may be possible my mother was no witch—'

'No more a witch than any other,' he replied. 'Though I speak of the flesh that bore me, I say that those who swore her life away are tainted with the blood of innocence—why, Kundre, lass, what aileth thee?'

The girl had flung her arms about him and was sobbing out her heart against his shoulder. For almost twenty years she'd led a pariah's life, hounded, scorned and persecuted, and the memory of her mother had been rubbed into her breaking heart like salt in a raw wound. Now here at last was one who had a kind word for her mother, who dared suggest she had not merited a felon's shameful death.

What happened then was like a chemical reaction in its spontaneity. It may have been that pity which is said to be akin to love inspired him to put his arms about her as she sobbed against his shoulder, but in the fraction of a heart-beat there was no questioning the emotion that possessed him. From him to her, and from her to him, there seemed to flow a mystic fluid—a sort of intangible soul-substance—that met and mingled like the waters of two rivers at their confluence and merged them into each other until they were not twain, but one.

It was an odd idyll, this romance of a man whose childhood had been spent in the house with a bawling woman and this woman whose whole life had been warped by hatred and suspicion. To say that they loved at first sight would not be accurate. Each had carried the image of the other in his heart since childhood, in each the thought of the other had been present constantly, not consciously, any more than they were conscious of the hearts that beat beneath their breasts, but always there, the greatest, most important, most vital thing in either of their lives. Now they were aware of it with blinding, dazzling suddenness. The glory of it almost stunned them.

Every evening when her work for Goody Stiles was done Kundre hurried to the oat field, and always he was there to greet her and come hurrying with uplifted hands to take her in his arms.

Judged by modern free-and-easy standards they were inhibited in their love-making. They hardly kissed at all, and when they did it was a chaste embrace which brother and sister might have exchanged. But she would put her hand in his and turn it till her soft palm rested on his and her little fingers made a soft and gentle pattern of his own, then rest her head against his shoulder till her gleaming hair was on his cheek, its perfume fresh and sweet as that of the green growing things about them.

I said theirs was an odd love. So it was. A love compounded partly of loneliness, partly of heart-hunger, partly of true, honest friendship; not without its moments of passion, but entirely without the savage, selfish hunger of passion; not lacking ecstasy, but with the ecstasy of love fulfilled, not satiated.

They did not talk much. There was small need of words, for that mysterious warm current, strong as a rising ocean tide, flowed constantly between them, fusing their two selves in one. And when they came to say good night the sweet pain of their parting was itself a compensation for the day-long separation facing them.

Then came catastrophe, as dreadful and as unexpected as a thunder-bolt hurled from a cloudless sky. Her brother Micah ran away from his master. It was either flight or murder, for despite the expert way in which he did his work old Goodman Belkton found fault with him constantly, and his fellow 'prentices, not slow to take their cue from the master, taunted him with his mother's conviction and intimated that he used her devilish arts to make his handiwork the best the 'walk turned out.

Runaway apprentices were fair game for anyone, and Goodman Belkton offered a reward of two pounds for the stray's return, so when four sturdy louts saw Micah on the dock at Salem Town, about to sign before the mast for a voyage in the Indies, they set on him and bound him with a length of rope and dragged him back to Danby.

But while they were still in the Danby suburbs they had been set upon by a ferocious heifer that gored one of them sorely, knocked down another, and put them all so utterly to flight that their prisoner escaped and joined his ship at Salem before she sailed with the tide. They brought their wounded comrade into Danby, where, over sundry mugs of potent rum-and-water, they had a wondrous story to relate.

The cow that set on them had been no ordinary cow, it seemed, but a demon beast whose nostrils breathed forth fiery flames, and which announced *in human words*, 'I'll soon set thee free from this scum, my brother!'

This all happened in the early evening, but before it was too dark for them to see the demon beast go tearing off across a meadow when its fell work had been done and suddenly sit down upon the sod like a woman, straddle a long fence-rail like a witch that mounts a broom, and fly shrieking off across the sky toward Goodman Stiles's oat field.

And where had Kundre been while this was happening? Her mistress asked her pointblank, and pointblank she refused to answer. And there the matter might have rested, perhaps, if Jonathan Sawyer, a labourer of Goodman Williams' plantation, had not volunteered the information that at nine o'clock the night before he's seen her hurrying from Stiles's oat field and heard her singing something not to be found in the hymn book.

It seemed hardly necessary for the constable to call a *posse comitans* of trained bandsmen to arrest her or to summon Parson Middleton to lend them spiritual assistance. But so he did, and with martial clank of sword and pike and musket, and with the Parson with his Book beneath his arm, they went to Goodwife Stiles's house and formally took Kundre into custody, bound her wrists together with the constable's spare bridle, put a horse's leading-strap about her neck and marched her through the streets to Danby jail, where they lodged her with a double guard before the door.

Hosea Newton roused from a deep, dream-tormented sleep, completely conscious, every faculty alert. His room was buried in a darkness blinding as a black cloak, for the moon had set long since, and a cloud-veil obscured the stars. Some instinct, some sentinel of the spirit that stands watch while we are sleeping, told him he was not alone, but he could see or hear nothing.

All day he'd raged through Danby Town like a madman, calling on the parson and the constable and even the high magistrate to intercede for Kundre. She was no witch, he vowed, but a sweet, pure maid who held his heart in the cupped palms of her two little hands. The ruffians who had told the story of the demon heifer were a lot of drunken, craven liars, seeking to excuse their prisoner's escape with this wild tale. He'd prove it; he would range the countryside until he'd found the cow that bested them and lead her singlehanded to the pound for all to see she was a natural beast.

The parson and the constable and magistrate were sympathetic listeners, but one and all refused to help in his trouble. The woman was a witch, the vowed and dedicated votary of Satan—like mother, like daughter. Could any natural cow put four strong men to flight, and they all armed with stout cudgels? And, most especially, could a natural beast bestride a fence-rail and sail through the sky on it? 'Poor boy, thou art bewitched by this vile whelp from Satan's kennels,' they told him.

'But fear not, poor, befuddled lad, tomorrow we shall prove that thy infatuation is the devil's work, for on the town common at sunrise we shall prick the witchling with long pins until we find the devil's mark, and thou shalt see she is in very truth a servant of the Prince of Darkness.'

He'd tried to see her in the jail, but the trained bandsmen turned him back. No one must see the witch until she had passed through the ordeal, even the turnkey was forbidden to go near her or to look into her cell. How should she eat and wherewith should she quench her thirst? Let Beelzebub her master see to that. They were Christian men and had no traffic with the servants of Satan.

Finally, worn out in body and in spirit, he had come home, refused his supper—could he take food while Kundre starved?—and thrown himself upon his bed, full-dressed, to fall into a sleep of utter exhaustion.

Desperate men make desperate plans, and Hosea was desperate. It did not matter to him whether she were good of bad or innocent or guilty. He loved her and would not desert her. If the court found her guilty—and accusation was equivalent to conviction—he would denounce himself as a wizard, and hang with her upon the gallows tree. She should not go to that dark land beyond the grave alone.

What was it? Something stirred in the soft darkness of the room; a shadow moving in the shadows, a rat that came to forage in the dark?

He knew that it was none of these, for in the gloom that blotted out the outlines of the furniture he saw a gleam of light, or rather lightness, like a cloud of faintly luminous vapour swirling from an unseen boiling kettle.

Slowly it spread, wafting upward, and now he saw the outlines of a figure in it, and the blood churned in his ears, his throat grew tight, and at the pit of his stomach he seemed to feel a burning and a freezing, all at once.

'Who—what art thou?' he croaked hoarsely, and the sound of his own frightened voice was terrifying in the haunted darkness.

No answer came to his challenge, but the figure looming faintly in the mist-cloud seemed taking on a kind of substance. Now he could see it quite clearly, and the terror which engulfed him seemed to be an icy flood that paralyzed his heart and brain and muscles.

Yet notwithstanding his terror he felt a kind of admiration for the phantom. It was a woman, tall as a tall man, yet with a calm and regal beauty wholly feminine. Across the low white brow a spate of gold-hued hair fell flowing to her knees, and from the perfect contour of her face great eyes of zenith-blue looked at him under brows of startling blackness. She was dressed in widow's weeds: a chain and pendant of some dull, lack-lustre metal hung about her throat.

He knew her! He has been a little lad scarce eight years old when Goodman Stiles had raised him to his shoulder that he might see the hangman Peter Grimes work the court's sentence on Kundre Maltby, the witch-woman. With a sudden pang of recollection he recalled how he had thought it a great pity that so much beauty should be vowed to Satan and hanged upon the gallows tree and entombed in the earth.

'What—' by supreme effort he forced speech between palsied lips—'what wouldst thou with me, Kundre Maltby?'

'Wilt take my help, Hosea Newton?' asked the spectre, and her voice was cold and desolate as December storm-wind blowing over pine-capped hills.

Hosea hesitated in his answer, and well he might. The wraith, if wraith it were, was that of a condemned witch-woman, hanged for sorcery, and, presumably, made fast in hell. He might have been in advance of his time, but he was part and parcel of his generation, and since Deuteronomy was penned men had regarded witches as disciples of the Evil One. To traffic with them was forbidden under pain of death and loss of soul. This was a witch's ghost, as dreadful as the witch herself, perhaps more dreadful, since she had burned in hell for twenty years, and he must make the choice of taking aid from her or bidding her begone. There was no middle course; he must hold true to all the teachings that had been instilled in him since infancy and bid her avaunt, or make compromise with Evil incarnate and put his soul in dreadful jeopardy—to what end? Did not the writings of the Fathers teach that Satan is the arch-deceiver? Would he keep the compact offered by this messenger from hell?

Then came the thought of Kundre, little Kundre, starved and thirsting, languishing in prison till the morrow, when they'd strip her to her shift in sight of all the town and pierce her tender flesh with long, cruel pins—a thousand thousand years of burning hell would be a bargain-price to pay for her deliverance.

'Say on, O spirit of my Kundre's mother,' he commanded. 'I'll take the help thou offerest me, and pay the price thou asketh.'

The phantom raised one white, almost transparent hand and loosed the medal from its neck. 'Take this,' it bade, and it seemed that its ghostly voice was stronger, warmer. 'Hie with it to the jail house and cut away the bars that pen her in. Then fly across the border southward—my time is sped, I must e'en go!'

The voice stopped suddenly, as though a hand had been laid on the spectre's throat, and like an April snowflake melting in the rising sun of spring, the faintly-shining vision merged back in the darkness.

He could not say if it had been a vivid dream or if a visitant had come to him, but presently he rose and struck a flint-spark in his tinderbox and lit a tallow dip. There on the floor beside his bed lay a medallion of dull metal, not lead nor iron, but apparently a mixture of the two, fixed to a length of slender chain of the same sheenless substance. Curiously, he noted that his hands were soiled with fresh earth and his fingernails broken, as though he had been burrowing like a woodchuck. Yet he knew he had not left his chamber since he flung himself upon the bed and fell asleep.

Or had he? We may wonder. Might he not have been the victim of somnambulism, and risen to go scraping at the earth that covered Kundre Maltby's body in the churchyard, then, still asleep, come back with the mysterious medal? The thought did not occur to him, but in the light of modern psychological experiments we may entertain it.

At any rate he recognized the medallion and took it in his hand. It was quite plain on one side and engraved with characters he could not read upon the other. Its edge was rounded like that of a milled coin, and though it was no larger than a penny it weighed as much as a gold sovereign.

What was it that the ghost had ordered him to do? Hie with it to the jail house and cut away the bars that pen her in.'

With this dull piece of soft metal? He was about to fling the medal from him in disgust when the echo of the ghostly voice seemed coming to him through the candlelight-stained darkness. 'Hurry, hurry, lover of the falsely-accused, or it will be too late!'

He knew what cell they'd lodged her in, the same in which her mother languished twenty years ago. It was on the ground floor of the prison, and by standing on his tiptoes he could look through the barred window.

If they caught him skulking round the jail house—What matter? He was resolved to die with her, why not share prison with her ere they hanged him?

Danby jail loomed dimly, a darker darkness in the starless night, as Hosea approached it, treading noiselessly in stockinged feet. 'Kundre,' he whispered softly as he tapped upon the stone sill of her cell window. 'Can'st hear me, dearest love?'

'Is't thou, my very dearest?' the girl's reply came to him through the formless darkness. 'Oh, Hosea—' He heard her sobs, the small, sad sounds of utter misery, as her voice broke.

'Aye, heart o' mine, 'tis I, and I have come to tell thee that thou shalt not go alone—come closer, love, stretch out thy hands to me—'

'I cannot, dearest one; they've chained me to the wall as if I were a rabid cur—'

Hosea clenched his teeth in fury and, unthinking, drove his hand against the prison bars. It was the hand in which he clasped the witch's medal, and as it struck the bar he drew back with a startled exclamation. The heavy, hand-forged iron had melted from contact with the medal as if it had been tallow touched by flame.

In a moment he was sawing at the window-bars with the mysterious coin, cutting them away as if they had been cheese. Silently he laid them on the turf outside the prison window, then, when he had an opening large enough to crawl through, let himself inside the cell and felt his way toward her.

They wasted no time in reunion or premature rejoicings. With her hand on his to guide it he pressed the witch's coin against the iron collar locked around her neck, and laid the fetter on the straw-strewn cell floor carefully, lest its clanking rouse the guard who waited in the corridor outside. Then, step by cautious step, he led her to the window.

Hand in hand they crept along the shadowed street until

they reached the stable where his mother's horses stamped before their mangers. In a moment he had saddled the best beast and led it out, swung her to the saddle-bow before him and set out toward the southern boundary of the town. They dared not trot or gallop lest the pounding of the horse's hoofs arouse the neighbours, but presently they reached the churchyard, and he drove his heels into the stallion's flanks.

'Wait, wait, my dear,' she begged him as they passed the white-spired meeting house, 'I would say farewell to my mother ere we shake the dust of Danby from our shoon forever.'

'Aye,' he conceded, lowering her to the ground. 'That is but fitting, sweetling. We are indebted to thy mother for thy liberty tonight.'

Together they walked to the grave, and while the girl knelt on the moss that rimmed the stone he looked down at her pensively. He wondered why his conscience did not trouble him. Tonight he had accepted diabolic aid, made compromise with Evil. Even now he had the witch-wife's medal in his pocket—he drew the flat metallic disc to look at it. Should he take it with him, or return it to the grave? he wondered, then wondered more at what was happening. The coin seem straining at his fingers, as if a thin, invisible thread were pulling it, or it had volition of its own and sought release from his grasp.

But, strangely, the pull was all in one direction, toward the foot of Kundre Maltby's grave.

Wonderingly, he stepped in the direction of the tug, and noticed that it increased sharply, then seemed to bear straight down toward the earth.

He dropped upon his knees. The coin seemed guiding his hand toward the tombstone and, still marvelling, he reached in the direction that it indicated. His fingers touched the long grass growing by the stone and found an opening like a woodchuck's burrow. Inside was something stiff and hard, yet slightly pliable, like old, oiled leather.

He grasped the object, tugged at it and brought it out. It was a leather sack, well smeared with tallow, stiff with age and long entombment in the earth, but wholly intact. A wax seal held the cord that bound its mouth, but this crumbled as he touched it. Inside were several smaller sacks, some of soft buckskin, some of coarse linen, and in them were bright English sovereigns, round silver Spanish dollars, and gleaming articles of jewellery. The mystery of Kundre Maltby's lost fortune was solved. She had buried it beneath the stone that marked her husband's empty grave, and when they went to scoop the hollow to receive her body they had used only the upper portion of the grave.

Hosea chuckled as he realized what has happened. The diggers' spades had been within a hand's-width of the treasure, yet none had suspected it.

Witchcraft? Perhaps, but very fortunate witchcraft for him and Kundre. A moment since they had had nothing but the clothes they stood in and the stolen stallion; now they were rich. Their life would not be hard—if they could get away.

The night was tiring rapidly as they rode into the woodland. Long streaks of grey were showing in the eastern sky, small noises came to them, the chirp of crickets and the sleepy murmurs of awakening birds, but on and on they rode, secure in the knowledge that Danby jail had no bloodhounds to pursue them, and their escape could not be known till sunrise, for no one, jailer or turnkey or guard, would dare go near the witch's cell till full daylight.

The Newport Quakers greeted them hospitably, and when they found that they had money offered them letters to the first citizens of Philadelphia.

In two days they took passage on a sloop bound for the Delaware, and, once on the high sea, were married by the master. So Kundre Maltby and Hosea Newton, children of seafaring Danby skippers, plighted troth upon the ocean, with the singing of the wind in the rigging for wedding march and the skirling mewl of sea gulls for a prothalamium.

They were not the first, nor, unhappily, the last to be driven from their homes by ignorance and bigotry masquerading as religion, but in Philadelphia they found such peace and happiness as never could have been theirs in New England. Their house stood on a tall hill overlooking the wide Schuylkill and the prosperous little Quaker city, and there their family multiplied until they had 'four sons and three daughters.

It was an evening in mid-April, the anniversary of her father's death at Captain Newton's hand, if she had known it, that Kundre stood with Hosea on the porch of their mansion and watched the lights of Philadelphia quench out against the darkness. Honora, their last-born daughter, had been christened in the afternoon, and now, all vestige of original sin washed from her, was slumbering as peacefully as any cherub in the nursery.

'Look, heart of mine,' bade Kundre, 'all those good folk go to their rest down yonder. They are a kind and gentle people, and I know their dreams are of a better world.'

'Aye, dearest,' he slipped an arm round her, 'a better world, in truth. Not in some dim, misty Promised Land on t'other side of Jordan, but here in this same world we live in. There'll come a time, my sweet, when men with lofty dreams shall waken at a great tomorrow's dawn and find their dreams still there, and nothing vanished but the night.'

The Bishop brought his story to a close and looked from Dr Bentley to the younger clergyman with a quizzical twinkle in his eye. 'I shan't ask you to pass judgement,' he said. 'Whether Hosea Newton should have scorned the witch's offer—or whether he received it, for that matter—are purely academic questions today. I'm pretty sure though,' he chuckled, 'that if he had refused it I should not be here this evening.'

'How's that, sir?' asked young Dr Kitteringson.

'Well, you see, Hosea Newton was my great-grandfather, several times removed, and his wife, the witch's child, my ancestress. So was the witch, for that matter.'

'And the witch's coin?' asked Dr Kitteringson. 'Do you know what became of it?'

'Yes,' answered Bishop Chauncey. 'Here it is.' He thrust two fingers in his waistcoat and produced a little metal disc which might have been silver, but it wasn't, flat and plain on one side, marked with faint traces of old Nordic runes upon the other. 'I've carried it as a lucky piece for years,' he added. 'My grandfather carried it all through the Civil War and never had a wound; my father had it with him at San Juan Hill and came off without a scratch. I lugged it through the Argonne and came out safely, but once when I left it on my dressing table in Paris I was run down by a taxi-cab before I had a chance to cross the street.'

Dr. Kitteringson was handling the strange coin gingerly, half curiously, half fearfully. 'You've tested it for magic powers?' he asked.

'Good gracious, no son. I don't suppose it has any, and— good heavens, look!'

Young Dr. Kitteringson had taken up the fire shovel and drawn the coin's blunt edge across its gleaming brass bowl. Where the medal touched the brass it cut a kerf as easily as if it had been pressed through softened tallow.

'Great Scott, Bishop—Dick!' exclaimed Dr Bentley. 'What do you think of that?'

The Bishop dropped the witch's coin back in his waistcoat pocket and held his glass out toward his host. His hand was shaking slightly, but his eyes and voice were steady. 'I think I'd like another drop of brandy; quickly, if you please,' he answered.

AUTHOR'S NOTE

Is the Devil a Gentleman? *is a question story. Whether Kundre Maltby was a witch at all, whether she appeared as a ghost to her future son-in-law, whether he actually compromised with evil or whether he was the victim of a vivid dream and a case of somnambulism—all these are questions which are continually raised through the course of the story.*

Like an advocate, I've merely presented the evidence in the case, but unlike an advocate, I've forhorn to argue from the evidence; hence the jury of readers must reach their verdict without help or hints from me.

Is the Devil a Gentleman?

Background for the story: Turn to page 117 of the Cambridge edition of the poems of John Greenleaf Whittier. There it all is, beautifully outlined for you, except for the Bishop, and the witch's coin and a few little things which I thought up myself.

SEABURY QUINN

49